D0437521

~ Purchased
with interest income
from the
library's trust fund ~

The Adventures of Benny and Watch

BENNY GOES INTO BUSINESS

COOKIES FOR SALE

Created by **Gertrude Chandler Warner**
Illustrated by **Daniel Mark Duffy**

ALBERT WHITMAN & Company
Morton Grove, Illinois

You will also want to read:

Meet the Boxcar Children
A Present for Grandfather
Benny's New Friend
The Magic Show Mystery

Library of Congress Cataloging-in-Publication Data

Warner, Gertrude Chandler, 1890-1979
Benny goes into business / created by Gertrude Chandler Warner;
illustrated by Daniel Mark Duffy.
p.   cm.
Summary: When Benny Alden decides he wants to go into business like
his grandfather, his first several attempts don't quite work out.
ISBN 0-8075-0637-0
[1. Moneymaking projects--Fiction.] I. Duffy, Daniel M., ill. II. Title.
PZ7.W244Bd   1999
[E]--dc21   98-33805
CIP
AC

Copyright © 1999 by Albert Whitman & Company.
Published in 1999 by Albert Whitman & Company,
6340 Oakton Street, Morton Grove, Illinois 60053.
Published simultaneously in Canada by
General Publishing, Limited, Toronto.

The Boxcar Children

Henry, Jessie, Violet, and Benny Alden are orphans. They are supposed to live with their grandfather, but they have heard that he is mean. So the children run away and live in an old red boxcar. They find a dog, and Benny names him Watch.

When Grandfather finds them, the children see that he is not mean at all. They happily go to live with him. And, as a surprise, Grandfather brings the boxcar along!

Almost every day after breakfast, Grandfather Alden said, "Good-bye. I'm off to business!" He kissed Jessie and Violet. He patted Henry on the back and hugged Benny.

One day, after Grandfather left, the children went out to the boxcar. Benny said, "I want to be in business, too."

"You have to think of what you like to do. That's the business to go into," Violet said.

Benny answered right away. "I like to EAT!"

"Well," Jessie said, laughing, "maybe you should try selling food."

"Cookies!" Benny shouted. "I'm going to bake and sell cookies!"

He ran back into the house.
"Mrs. McGregor, I'm going into
business. I'm going to bake cookies
and sell them in the neighborhood.
Will you help me?"

"Of course," Mrs. McGregor said. "Where will you sell them? At a stand?"

"Good idea. But first I have to bake them. Peanut butter cookies! That's what I want to sell. Peanut butter cookies."

Mrs. McGregor got out all the ingredients. She and Benny measured them into a big bowl. Benny started stirring.

"This is hard work," he said.

"You just keep mixing. I'll be back in a few minutes. I have to mail a birthday card to my niece," Mrs. McGregor said.

Suddenly, Benny heard his friend
Michael calling, "Come on out!"

Benny ran outside and said to Michael,
"I'm starting a cookie business. Come in
and help me bake them."

The boys went back inside.

"Oh, no!" Michael said.

"Watch!" Benny shouted. "What have you done?"

"He ate all the batter. *That's* what he's done!" Michael said.

Michael went home, and Benny sat on the steps. Mrs. Kramer, the Aldens' next-door neighbor, came over.

"I'm glad you're here, Benny. How would you like to do a little job for me?"

"Sure," Benny said. "What is it?"

"Come over to my house and I'll show you," said Mrs. Kramer.

In the kitchen, Mrs. Kramer picked up her cat. "You know Minnie. I'm going away tomorrow for a couple of days, and I need someone to feed her. Of course, I'll pay you."

"All right!" Benny said.
"I'm in business again.
The cat-sitting business!"

The next morning when Grandfather said, "I'm off to business," Benny laughed and said, "I'm off to business, too."

He ran next door and opened the door with the key Mrs. Kramer had given him. Inside he called, "Minnie! Minnie!" But there was no cat.

Benny heard a clock ticking, a faucet dripping, a floorboard creaking, but no meows from Minnie.

He went into the
kitchen and looked
in the cupboard.
No Minnie.

He went into every
room and looked in
every corner.

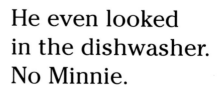

He even looked
in the dishwasher.
No Minnie.

Had Minnie run away? Just then
Henry came running into the house.
"Mrs. Kramer called. She said that
since she will only be away for two
days, she decided to take Minnie with
her," he said.

"I guess that's the end of my
cat-sitting business," Benny said.

Benny walked back home, looking sad. Mrs. McGregor was in her garden, picking some tomatoes. "What's wrong?" she asked.

"Mrs. Kramer took Minnie with her, so I'm out of business again."

Mrs. McGregor thought for a minute. "This garden needs watering very badly. How about going into the gardening business? You can start tomorrow."

"Wow," Benny said. "I can't wait."

But when Benny woke up the next morning, he heard something that made him shout, "Oh, no!"

Rain was beating on the roof. Big fat
raindrops were falling all over the lawn
and the garden.

He ran down to the kitchen. "It's raining! That's another job I've lost," Benny said.

"Sit down and have some breakfast," Grandfather said. "We'll think of something else for you to do."

"I'm not hungry," Benny said. "I'll just go back to my room." But he took a big doughnut with him before he left the kitchen.

Benny was looking at his baseball cards when his friend Beth ran into his room.

"Hi, Benny," she said. "My mom is taking me to town to buy a birthday card for my aunt. Want to come?"

Benny shrugged. "I don't know . . ."

And then he laughed. "Cards! Cards! Everyone needs cards. That's the business for me. I'll make greeting cards."

The next day in the boxcar, Benny said, "You know, it's good to have partners, because our greeting card business is going to be a big success."

"Right!" Michael and Beth said at the same time.